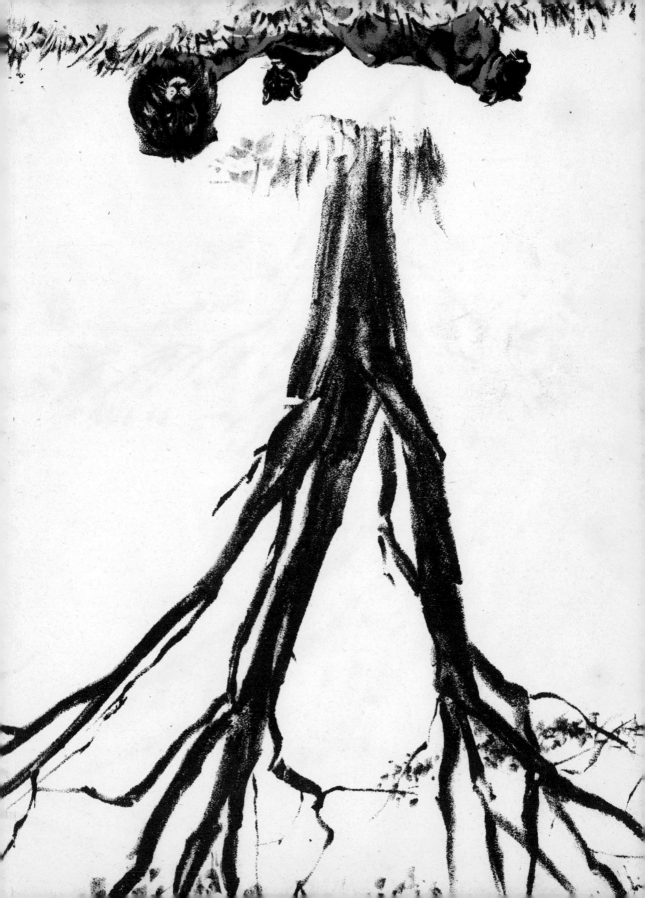

Munya the Lion.

MUNYA the LION

by Dorothy Martin

decorations by

Joan Kiddell-Monroe

OXFORD ~ UNIVERSITY ~ PRESS
London ~ ~ New York ~ ~ Toronto

The meaning of words used in South Africa
which occur in this story:

Ngon, pronounced Ingon, short for Ngonyama, the native word
    for lion.

Bushveld, bush country.

Veld, wild open country.

Kopje, pronounced koppy, a hill.

Wildbeeste, pronounced vilderbeast, wild cattle.

Induna, pronounced Indoona, leader.

Impala, a buck, an animal rather like a deer, but having no spots.

12659

Near the lily-pool

This is the story of Munya the lion.

There is a great Game Reserve in South Africa, a place set apart for wild animals, where they are perfectly safe from man, and where no one may hunt or kill them. It was here that Munya was born.

It was spring time. The funny little neat looking trees dotted about the *bushveld,* which never seem able quite to grow up, were hurrying into their new green suits. Little fresh blades of grass were springing up everywhere. There were flowers growing too—blue, white and yellow.

It was the happiest time in the year, and the busiest because nearly everyone seemed to be having babies. Ingala, a lovely young lioness, had one. She had made a small clearing in a reed-bed near a lily-pool, and had beaten down a narrow track between thorn-bushes and long grass, by which she could go in and out. This clearing was to be her home or lair, and there early one morning Munya, her first cub, was born.

He had a funny little puckered face, with rather a worried expression. That was perhaps because he couldn't see. His eyes would not be open for ten days or so, like a kitten's. He was a soft greyish-yellow colour. His little head was almost square, with tiny furry ears,

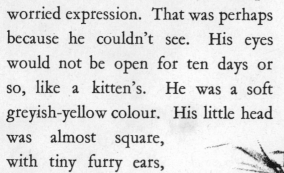

and his legs were so shaky that he could hardly stand. It was difficult to believe that anything so small and helpless could ever become a magnificent, full-grown lion.

He squeaked once or twice, just one or two little faint, fretful squeaks as much as to say: "I don't like this; it's such a strange dark world."

But Ingala kissed him with a soft, comforting tongue, and purred and purred like a great contented cat. "Wurr-urr-urr," she crooned, deep down in her throat, "wurr-urr-urr, my cub, my baby."

Then she licked him all over from tiny nose to tail. She lay down when she had finished, and Munya, nestling close up to her, began to like his strange dark world after all.

The day was nearly over and night was drawing on. A little breeze had sprung up. The birds round the lily-pool were singing their evening chorus. The chorus seemed fuller and happier than usual, as if the birds were pleased and proud to have a lion cub near their lily-pool, a royal baby. The lion is the king of beasts, you see, so that the little Munya was a royal prince.

The sun, a great ball of gold, was slipping down behind a purple mountain; it would soon be dark. Frogs began croaking and rattling at the edge of the lily-pool. Ingala grumbled at them, afraid that they might wake her baby who was fast asleep, curled up beside her. Night-jars churred. Hyenas laughed and whined. *Wildebeeste* coughed, the way they do, keeping their little ones very near them.

The tiny Munya, hearing none of these sounds, snuggled up close to his mother.

Lions roared in the distance. Ingala raised her head

6

and listened. The roaring drew nearer, roar upon roar—the wild animals' thunder.

"They're hunting," growled Ingala, standing up, "and killing. I'm hungry. I must go out and join them."

She stole down the narrow track. Munya stirred a little, then slept on peacefully, safe in the lair.

II.

Munya tastes flesh for the first time

Though Munya belonged to a royal family, the lair could hardly be called a palace. It was too simple a place for that, with its bare floor and reed walls.

Below it lay the lily-pool, where pink and white water-lilies floated like fairy boats, and lily-trotters, brownish-yellow birds with long toes and claws, stepped from flower to flower, screaming at each other.

Ingala was very busy looking after her son, feeding him, putting him to bed, waking him up, patting him, rolling him over with her big paw, and washing him. She was so anxious to have him perfectly clean, that she actually gave him a bath one day. She picked him up by his neck and carried him down the narrow track to where there was a little pool of water. She held him dangling over it. It really looked as if she might be going to drown him. But all she did was to dip him gently once or twice in the water, Munya sniffling and squeaking. Then she

7

carried him safely back to the entrance of the lair, where she put him down to dry in the sun.

Sometimes she had to leave him for a little while when she went out in search of food.

One day when he was alone, wobbling about the lair, trying to amuse himself, he suddenly had a bright idea.

"I'll go a little way along the track," he thought, "and look out for my mother." His eyes were open by now of course.

He crept cautiously through the opening to the lair, then stood still for a moment. The reeds seemed very tall, but when he looked up he could just see the blue sky far above him. He went on a little way, then his courage failed him, and he dared go no farther by himself. He was such a *little* cub, and there were so many new sounds which frightened him: rustlings and cracklings, splashings in the lily-pond and things moving. He cried a little and miaowed. He wanted his mother. It seemed such a long time since she left him.

Suddenly he stopped crying, and listened, cocking his little ears. He sniffed. "What's that scent?" he asked himself. He sniffed again. "Mother!" he squeaked, scenting her, "Mother!"

It *was* Ingala. She came rustling and pushing her way between the reeds, down the narrow track. She was carrying a small dead buck in her jaws, dragging it under her body between her front legs. She dropped the buck just outside the entrance to the lair, and panting, she called Munya to her.

"Flesh!" she growled. "Buck, Munya."

Then she tore off a small piece of rounded bone, with

Munya sat waiting at the opening to the lair.

a very little meat on it, and put it down in front of him. He sniffed at it, patted it, then picked it up and carried it into the lair. He held it between his paws and gnawed and sucked it until his little face was red with blood. This was the first time he had tasted flesh, and he thought how juicy and good it was.

Ingala looked on with her amber-coloured eyes. Her great head with its little white beard and whiskers seemed almost to fill up the entrance to the lair.

When Munya had finished his little bit, she fell upon the buck herself, and made a good meal off it. Then she went right into the lair and licked her paws. When they were clean she began to wash Munya. She held him down with her paw and licked him hard with her tongue.

"Oh, oh!" he squealed. "You hurt, Mother, you hurt."

"It can't be helped," rumbled Ingala, licking away harder than ever. "Anything is better than a dirty little cub. There now, you're nice and clean again."

She lay down and Munya began playing with the black tuft at the end of her tail. It made such a lovely plaything. Ingala watched him with pride, purring contentedly.

Then Munya, beginning to feel sleepy after his meal, plumped his little body down across his mother's front paws, and rubbed his face lovingly against her chin. She kissed him, just one or two soft licks. Munya cuddled up close to her and dropped off to sleep. Ingala dozed, but at the slightest sound from outside she was wide awake and growling softly.

She must protect her baby from all harm, he was so small and helpless, and she was so big and strong.

III.

A storm

The days passed and Munya grew bigger and stronger. He could go out with Ingala now, and sometimes Ngon his father would join them. Ngon was a handsome, kingly-looking young lion with a thick black mane. Munya much admired him, and was proud to be able to walk out with his father.

One day Ngon and Ingala threw themselves down, panting, under a wild fig tree. It was midday and very hot, too hot to move. They dozed off to sleep, their fawn-coloured bodies almost hidden in long cool grass. Munya slept too, close to his parents.

He woke after a while, sat up and yawned. He had grown to look rather like a large, soft teddy-bear, only he was a paler colour, and had pretty dark spots on his legs and tummy.

He glanced around, wondering what he could do to amuse himself. He looked up at the branches of the fig tree, spreading one above the other over his head. What fun it would be to climb right to the top of the tree and look out at everything between the leaves.

Munya began scrambling and pulling himself up on to the lowest branch. There he stuck. He couldn't get to the one above, the branches were too far apart. He wobbled and shook, and the branch he was on cracked under his weight, broke, and he found himself sprawling on the ground. He picked himself up, and looked round to see what his parents were doing. They still lay stretched in the grass sound asleep.

Now Munya had always longed to know what his father's mane felt like. He had never dared touch it, but now was his chance. He crept up to Ngon and with his small paw gently patted the coarse black hair. Nothing happened. Munya, becoming bolder, tried to pull out some of it to play with. He chewed a bit of the mane too. It was rather nice stuff to chew. Ngon grunted: "Umm-umm, ugh, ugh." He had not been so fast asleep after all then. Much annoyed, he raised himself, growling, lifted his great paw and cuffed Munya, knocking him over flat.

Munya screamed, lay still for a moment, then stood up, gave himself a little shake and moved farther away from his parents.

Then the wind got up. Thunder boomed and rolled in the distance like big guns. Ngon came out from under the tree. He lashed his black-tipped tail, threw open his great jaws and roared: "Oo-oo-oo-ugh-ugh, rah-*oom*, rah-*oom*! A storm! Imbulu! Evil one!"

Lions hate storms. Ngon knew that one was coming. He heard it and scented it. So did Ingala who stood sniffing the air. The thunder drew nearer. Lightning flashed and zigzagged. Ingala called to Munya and they hurried back to the lair. Ngon followed and crouched down between some big rocks, frowning at the black clouds which had gathered overhead. The wind, roaring and rushing, swept over the reed-bed, almost bending the reeds double. The rain came down in torrents. The sun seemed to have gone to the other end of nowhere, so dark had it become.

Little streams of water pushed their way into the reed-bed and oozed up into the lair.

"Miaow, miaow," squeaked Munya, crawling right under his mother for safety, "miaow, miaow." This was his first storm and he was frightened. At last it passed over, leaving everything clean and sparkling.

Father lion came to the entrance to the lair, grumbling. They would have to move their home as the summer rains seemed to have begun, though much earlier than usual. It would never do to stay in the reed-bed: it lay too low. It was sad to leave the lair. Ingala had been very happy there with Munya, her first cub. It had been safe and cosy. They would have to try and find a nice dry place on some *kopje*. There was Baboonkop of course, a favourite *kopje*, but it might be difficult to find room there as it was so popular with lion families that time of year. However, Ngon decided to take his little family to Baboonkop and try their luck.

Besides, the rest of the pride to which they belonged might be there, and it was time they joined up with it again. Munya would have plenty of cub relations then to play with. He was bouncing about now like a puppy, round and round the lair, out a little way and in again.

"When do we start?" he squealed.

"To-morrow at dawn," rumbled father lion, "rah-*oom*, rah-*oom*."

IV

Baboonkop

Baboonkop, where Munya's father and mother hoped to find a new home, is a rocky hill, where trees and lovely flowering shrubs grow. It is called Baboonkop because so many baboons live there. There are caves to hide or to sleep in, and all kinds of funny-shaped spiny cacti growing between the rocks.

It is really like a great block of flats, a different animal family living on each floor.

Klipspringers, little plump light brown buck, have the top flat. Below are the baboons, and on the ground-floor lions. There they have a favourite lair, where time after time cubs are born, gradually open their eyes and go out with their mothers, just as Munya had done.

Of course you can't expect baboons to keep to their own flat, they are far too restless and fond of making friends. They are all over the place, up at the top calling on the klipspringers with whom they have always been very friendly, sitting in the trees, chattering, quarrelling, pulling each other's tails and swinging from the branches. They are careful not to go too near the lion's flat, however, when they know that they are at home.

Early one morning Klip, one of the klipspringers, was breakfasting off delicious little fresh blades of grass at the top of the *kopje*. Springer, her husband, was keeping watch on a large square rock. He stood so still, and looked so stiff, he might have been a little figure carved in wood or stone, not made to move at all. One or other of them always kept watch like that. You see any-

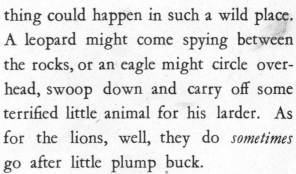

thing could happen in such a wild place. A leopard might come spying between the rocks, or an eagle might circle overhead, swoop down and carry off some terrified little animal for his larder. As for the lions, well, they do *sometimes* go after little plump buck.

Suddenly Springer leapt off the rock. He wanted *his* breakfast too. He felt that Klip had been long enough over hers. She was a good little wife and seemed to understand. She sprang on to the rock and stood there perfectly still, looking out across the *bushveld*.

Lower down the *kopje* Moko and Bafana, two little baboons, were having a great time. They had breakfasted well off scorpions which their mothers had found for them under some loose stones. Before letting the little ones eat the scorpions, they had pulled off the ends of their tails which have poisonous stings.

A little way off Minung, a big baboon, was sitting on the Pulpit Rock, a huge rock called thus because of its shape, which is like one of those high round pulpits which you see in some churches.

Minung sat at the top, silently looking out across the *bushveld* to distant blue hills, keeping watch. He had done this for years and was the best watchman that troop of baboons had ever had. Nothing escaped his wise old eyes. He was their leader, too, and with his council of eleven old baboons, he saw to it that the laws of the baboons were duly kept.

"Look," chuckled Moko, scratching his little tummy, "there's old Minung sitting up there. Let's see if we can get some fun out of him."

They crept up behind Minung.

"Anyone at home?" squeaked Bafana, tapping on the baboon's broad back. No answer.

Not in the least discouraged, Moko scrambled up Minung's back and began tickling his ears. Still Minung took no notice. Bafana tried to bite him with his little sharp white teeth, but he couldn't get very far with that; Minung's skin was too rough and scarred under the matted hair.

Then suddenly Minung let himself fall backwards, pretending to be very, very tired. Moko and Bafana, screaming with delight, sprang on to the old fellow and began jumping about on his hairy chest.

But Minung was clever. He lay still for a little while, and let them enjoy themselves.

Then, sitting up suddenly, he grabbed each little imp by the scruff of the neck, and carried them to a pool of water among the rocks and ducked them both in it head-first. He was fond of young baboons and thought it all a good joke, but he wanted to teach them not to be *too* cheeky to their elders.

"Ow-ow!" squealed Moko.

"Oh-oh!" screamed Bafana.

They gasped and struggled until Minung set them on their feet again. They ran off, chattering and crying, and clambered up the *kopje* to their mothers, whose deep anxious voices were calling to them.

Klipspringers and baboons lived in the top flats

Minung went back to the Pulpit Rock, and sat there perfectly still, with no sort of expression on his long wooden-looking face. Suddenly a little quiver ran through his big body. He sat up straighter and listened. He had heard a distant rumbling, and the sound drew nearer.

"Ngonyama!" he muttered to himself, "Ngonyama! Lions!"

Presently he saw figures coming across the *veld*, stealing cautiously between the trees and bushes. As gradually they came nearer, he made out what they were: a big black-maned lion, a lioness and a little cub. It was Munya and his father and mother.

Now lions with cubs must not be annoyed or interfered with, as they may become dangerous, imagining some harm to their babies. Minung stood up and, with loud harsh barks, warned his troop of baboons that lions with a cub were on their way to Baboonkop, and that they must be careful.

Numbers of baboons appeared on the *kopje*: big baboons, middle-sized baboons, little baboons, all barking.

The lion family came nearer, Munya walking between his parents.

Just then there came an angry roar from the ground-floor of Baboonkop, and Imbube, an old brown-maned lion, came out on to the road which runs round the *kopje*, switching his tail and sniffing the air. With him were several lionesses and five cubs. Imbube knew from the barking of the baboons that more lions must be coming towards Baboonkop. He was the king, or leader of this pride which lived and hunted in its own territory round about the *kopje*.

If the new-comers were strangers the lions of the pride

would fight them and drive them away. They would not have outsiders in their territory, hunting their game and perhaps trying to take possession of their land.

Imbube and the lionesses strode on to the *veld;* a little army all ready to fight if necessary.

Ngon came on slowly, leaving Ingala and Munya a little way behind.

The baboons on the *kopje,* barking and chattering, gathered together in little groups to watch. They would enjoy looking on at a good fight between the lions if there was one. Mother baboons carried their babies higher up the *kopje* for safety. The five cubs, warned by their mothers, hid under some bushes.

But as they drew nearer to each other the two lions discovered that they *did* belong to the same pride and all was well. Imbube was satisfied and there was no fight. But he raised his head and thundered : " Oo-oo-oo, ugh-ugh-rah-oom, rah-oom," as if to remind them all that he was still their king and leader, and that only *one* king can rule at a time.

The five cubs came out from under the bushes, and Munya tumbled headlong through the long grass in his hurry to get to them.

They began romping like kittens rolling each other over, hiding and jumping out, arching their backs and charging at each other : six cubs with such innocent expressions on their little faces that it was difficult to believe how naughty and mischievous they really were.

This had been a great day for Munya; the day he and his parents joined the pride, the day he first met his cub relations.

V.

What Munya saw

One day the pride left Baboonkop to spend the afternoon on another big *kopje* near by. There was more room for the lions there to spread themselves out on the rocks in the sun, which they loved doing.

Lions, lionesses and cubs, joined by a number of bigger cubs, strolled across the *veld* to the other *kopje*. It took quite a long time to get there because the cubs would keep stopping to play. They straggled about like sheep, and had to be collected again.

At last they reached the *kopje* and climbed up its rocky side. They lay down, sprawling in the sun, a mass of yellowish-brown. But Munya, hot though it was, did not wish to go to sleep. He wanted to see things. He had become quite an inquisitive, plucky little cub by now. So he sat by himself on a rock lower down.

Kiewiets flew screeching over his head, noisy white-capped birds with orange-coloured legs. Some giraffe, their heads showing above the trees, moved across the *veld* at a gentle canter, anxious to get farther away from the lions, and to find a place where they could have their suppers—bunches of leaves and buds off the trees—in peace. The giraffe moved in such a funny way, slowly up and down, up and down, rather as if they were in a slow-motion picture.

From where he sat Munya could see a road, winding across the *bushveld* from the blue hills. Presently something

21

came along it, bright and glistening in the hot sunshine. Like the tall giraffe it had a funny way of moving. It rolled along on four round legs. Munya growled. He had seen quite a number of animals already in his short life, but never one like this. A second shiny thing appeared on the road and a third. They soon reached the *kopje*, hummed slowly round it and stopped just below Munya. He stared at the queer-looking things, his eyes growing rounder and rounder with astonishment. More astonishing still were the animals sitting inside the queer things, who stared back at Munya, and made funny, talking noises. He got up, snarled and, feeling a little nervous, thought he would go to his mother. He found her asleep, flat on her back.

"Miaow, miaow, Mother," he cried, waking her up. "Such funny things on the road!"

Ingala rolled over, stood up and stretched herself. She looked down at the cars, but without much interest; she had seen so many. Thousands go into this great Game Reserve every year, taking visitors from all over the world to see the wild animals in their own kingdom.

Cubs are interested in them, of course, when they first see them, though a little frightened just as Munya was. The lions get some fun out of them sometimes, as you will see.

"Umm-umm," rumbled Ingala, "motor car things!"

"And the animals inside them?" growled Munya.

"Men animals, but they won't do us any harm, Munya. We're safe in our own Reserve."

It was time now for the pride to make a move. One by one the lions rose, slowly climbed from rock to rock to the top of the *kopje* and down the other side, which was the direction

of their drinking place. They found the three motor cars drawn up in the road, waiting for them.

The cubs, much interested, sat down in rows, one behind the other by the roadside and gazed at the queer things, as if they were at a theatre, watching a good show.

Presently the lions and bigger cubs began to prowl round the cars. One cub played with a buffer; he liked its hard brightness. Another quietly tried to nibble a tyre. A third stood up on his hindlegs, rested his front paws against the door of one of the cars, and looked in. The men animals inside quickly jerked up the window and the cub dropped down into the road.

Then very slowly the cars began to move, making their way carefully through the crowd of lions.

Suddenly Imbube and Ngon stepped into the middle of the road behind the cars. Lions can be playful if they are in the mood. From the expressions on their faces it was clear that Imbube and Ngon *were* in the mood.

"Oo-oo-oo, ugh-ugh-rah-*oom*, rah-*oom*!" they roared and began to follow the cars. The lionesses and cubs kept up with them as best they could. The lions knew perfectly well that they need only chase the motor car things a short distance in order to have the fun of seeing them bolt like frightened hares.

The cars went faster, the lions still following. But when the cars began to move really quickly, Imbube called a halt. He knew that they couldn't keep up any longer. He sat down in the middle of the road, panting, his great tongue lolling out. Pleased at having chased the motor car things so successfully, he looked round proudly, so proudly that he might have been king of the *whole* Reserve, instead of king of just a small portion of it.

After resting a little while, the lions turned and strolled off to their drinking place.

VI.

The open space.

Induna, the *impala,* came trotting out into an open space, which had trees and bushes all round it, and tempting looking little paths, leading away through tangled thorn bushes and long grass. Induna had splendid horns and was a lovely reddish-brown colour. He stood quite still, his head raised, listening.

Among the trees behind him yellow-brown figures moved, a big herd of *impala,* waiting to do whatever Induna, their scout and leader, ordered them.

Induna turned his head this way and that, until he caught the wind in his face. Then, not liking the scent it brought him, he trotted back a little way and barked: "Danger! Come on."

Induna rushed back into the open space.

Leaves rustled, branches cracked—broke, and the whole herd rushed out and dashed across the open space. Leaping and bounding, they disappeared among the trees opposite.

Induna waited for a few moments. Then, when a booming sound rang out—a roar—he leapt forward and tore after the others.

Under a shady mahogany tree, within sight of the open space and watching all this, lay Ingala with the six cubs. She had been told off to look after them, so that the other mothers might be left free to go out hunting. She stood up, switching her tail.

"Umm-umm," she growled, "a hunt! a kill!"

From a distance came short, whining barks: "A-bow-wow-*wow*-wow-wow-*wow*." Jackals were calling to one another, and rounding up, ready to follow the hunt.

The cubs pricked their ears. Then they heard another sound, a sound they knew well, Ngon and Imbube roaring: "Oo-oo-oo-ugh-ugh, rah-*oom*, rah-*oom*." Ingala lashed her tail.

Just then Induna rushed back into the open space, and stood for a moment, panting, his eye on a far corner where there was a small gap between the bushes. He tore off and darted through it. Immediately Ingala, good huntress that she was, knew what she ought to do. She ought to go and drive him round, back to where the lions must be. Otherwise he might get away.

Ingala was young and full of life. It was going to be a great hunt. She couldn't *bear* to miss it. The cubs would be safe enough under the mahogany tree.

"Stay here, cubs," she rumbled. "Don't move from this place, and I'll come back for you."

She started off. The cubs watched her going cautiously

but quickly, down one side of the open space, disappearing through the gap at the far corner.

Munya looked out longingly at the open space. Some day he would be big enough to go off on his own, the way young lions do, just wherever he chose.

"Your mother won't forget to come back for us, Munya, will she?" whimpered little Impeta, the weakest one. "She brought us so far, we couldn't find our way home without her."

"She won't forget," growled Munya.

It was all very quiet. The lions must have gone a long way hunting as the cubs couldn't hear them any more.

"Oh, I'm so hungry," mewed little Impeta.

"So am I, so am I," whined all the others.

The day wore on and it was getting late. The sun was going down, golden-red, behind the trees.

The cubs didn't know what to do. They were so *dreadfully* hungry. It seemed such a long time since Ingala had left them, and it was almost dark. At last they thought they would venture out just a little way to see if there was any sign of her, though they knew they ought not to leave the mahogany tree.

"Oh, I'm frightened, I'm frightened," cried Impeta, "it'll soon be *quite* dark."

But Munya was not afraid. He stepped out bravely into the open. It was not dark there at all because the moon had just risen above the trees.

The six small cubs wandered miserably round the open space, peering down each little path, hoping to see Ingala stealing along one of them. But it was no good. She did not come.

They went back to their tree at last.

"I'm tired, I'm tired," cried Kulu the fattest cub, flinging himself down, "and *so* hungry."

"We *all* are," whimpered the others, " so, so hungry."

They curled themselves round as close to each other as they could.

The wind sprang up, and brought with it two big, white-edged clouds, which spread themselves out like the wings of an angel, watching over the cubs.

VII.

The third day

Dawn broke, the darkness lifting like a curtain all round, and there was the great Game Reserve again.

Munya opened his eyes, yawned and wondered where he was. He stared up at the branches overhead, and suddenly he remembered.

The others woke up too, and they all peeped out at the open space. *Wildebeeste* were grazing there now and plump, beautifully striped zebra. Some of them had babies which looked so clean and fresh that they might have been brand-new toys just out of a toy shop. They frisked about, kicking up their little heels, and running up to their mothers to be fed.

"They're all having breakfast," grumbled Kulu.

"All except us," miaowed Impeta.

"Couldn't we catch one of those little ones," grunted Kulu softly, "and — eat it?"

"No," growled Munya, "we don't know how to catch them, and if we tried, they'd all run away, and we might not be able to find our way back here again if we followed them."

It grew hot, and the *wildebeeste* and zebra wandered off among the trees to shelter from the sun.

A road ran behind the mahogany tree. The cubs ventured out and took a little walk up and down it, looking for Ingala, but they dared not go far. They soon went back to their tree; it was a home to them now. But they were getting terribly hungry, and thirsty too. Kulu was thinner already, and his figure much improved.

The river close by had dried up; there had been no rain for a long time, and the cubs didn't know their way to the nearest waterhole.

Munya looked out anxiously for his mother, his kittenish face worried and frowning. But Ingala did not come that day, nor did she the next. But the third day something happened. A motor car thing came humming along the road with men animals inside it as usual.

The cubs struggled to their feet and snarled. If they had been strong enough they would have run away and hidden

among the bushes. They were still a little frightened of motor cars.

The car drew up just opposite the mahogany tree. The men gazed at the cubs, and saw how weak and starved-looking they were.

The cubs heard them talking in their funny language. Then they went off quickly the way they had come. After some time they came back, but in a different kind of motor car thing, a lorry. The men drove it close up to the tree, let down the back and, lo and behold, a dead buck fell out on to the grass. The ranger, or guardian, who looks after that part of the Reserve, had shot it for them, a thing that only a ranger may do.

The cubs sniffed a smell they knew, a good smell, a food smell.

Almost before the body had reached the ground, they had fallen upon it, and were tearing at the flesh and eating it. Even little Impeta managed to suck a tiny bit. Soon their faces were red with blood and there was nothing left but a few bones.

Then the men, knowing how thirsty the cubs must be, brought a zinc bath filled with water, and quietly put it on the ground, hoping that the cubs would come and drink. But nothing would make them go near the bath; they were far too nervous. It seemed such a queer, dangerous looking thing to them.

The men knew that the cubs *must* have water, so they thought of another plan. They went off again and came back with some large basins. They dug holes in the ground, in which they sank them. Then they filled the basins with water and went and stood a little way off to see what would happen.

The cubs sniffed and smelt, and very cautiously stole up to where the basins were. They couldn't see them now of course as they were in the ground, but—they saw the *water*. They purred and purred: "Little waterholes! Little waterholes!" It was a sort of miracle, suddenly to find water where there had not been a drop. They lapped and lapped as if they would never stop. All but Impeta, who was too exhausted to move.

Then one of the men, seeing how weak and helpless he was, came quietly across the grass, bent down and picked him up. Impeta spat and struggled a little, but the man spoke gently to him and quieted him, then carried him to the motor car. The car thumped and whirred, started off along the road and disappeared in a cloud of dust.

You need not worry about Impeta. The men who took him away must have looked after him well, because if you visit one of the great zoos you will find a splendid lion there, whom everyone admires. His name now is Leo, but *once* it was Impeta, the weakest one.

The five cubs stared stupidly after the lorry. Then, feeling very sleepy after their huge meal, they crept under the mahogany tree and fell fast asleep. Kulu's figure, I must tell you, was as fat as it was before.

At nightfall Munya stirred, and, half asleep, he thought of his mother. He was well fed and comfortable now, but still he wanted her. He longed to snuggle up close to her, to press his little soft body against her big warm one.

The moon was full and it was all very quiet except for a few animal grunts and the chirrupping of tiny insects.

Then, from a distance, came another sound—a soft anxious call—and a dark figure came slowly along the dry river-bed.

The call drew nearer: "Croo-oo-*oo*, croo-oo-*oo*."

31

Wide awake now, Munya sat up and listened. "My mother!" he cried and ran out into the open.

The others woke up, too, and rushed after him. They stood, listening, sniffing, and at last down one of the little paths in the moonlight came Ingala, limping.

The cubs all ran to her and talked and purred. She and Munya sniffed noses and she kissed him with her tongue.

It had been a long hunt it seemed. Induna had got away after all and the lions had killed a *wildebeest* instead. Ingala had hurt her leg badly and had not been able to come to them before. She limped to the mahogany tree and wearily threw herself down under it. The cubs curled themselves round her as happy as they could be.

"Wurr-urr-urr," she purred, "wurr-urr-urr."

She took them back to Baboonkop the next day.

VIII.

The first hunting lesson and a kill

Time passed and Munya, who had nearly reached his second birthday, was old enough to begin his training in hunting and killing. His parents had chosen the dry river-bed as a suitable place for his first lesson. There was a pool of water left in one place where all kinds of animals came down to drink.

Ngon and Ingala lay on one bank of the river-bed, near the edge, peering between the reeds. On the opposite

Ingala returns, lin

bank Munya and the other four cubs, who had been invited to share the lesson, were hidden under some bushes. They sat watching, listening, and quivering if there was the slightest sound. At any moment some animal might come down to the pool to drink.

For a little while nothing happened. Then a zebra appeared on the bank opposite Ngon and Ingala. He was a nice plump zebra with dark stripes. Some more came up behind him and they all stood timidly waiting to see if it was safe to go down to the pool. At last some of them ventured. But they hesitated when they were halfway down the sandy bank. Something must have startled them. They backed into each other, turned and dashed up the bank again.

Ngon and Ingala watched, crouching. Another little party of zebra, braver than the others, came right down into the river-bed, glanced round, then stepped cautiously to the pool and began to drink.

Suddenly Ngon and Ingala sprang down the bank into the river-bed. Now was their chance to drive the zebra towards the place where the cubs were in hiding. The cubs knew what to do then. They were to come out quietly, go towards the zebra, or any other animal driven that way by the lions, separate one from the rest if possible and chase it as far as they could. They were to try and start a hunt in fact.

But they made such a rustling noise as they came out from under the bushes, and did it all so clumsily, that the zebra were off and away before the cubs could get anywhere near them.

In the meantime Ngon and Ingala had gone back to their place on the bank. They themselves had no intention of hunting that day. It was the cubs' day, and a very important one, too.

The cubs stood looking rather silly, not knowing what to do next. But Ngon went over to them.

"Badly done," he growled. "Get under the bushes and try again." He stole back to Ingala.

It was very hot. The pool in the river-bed was the nearest drinking place, so when there were no lions to be seen, the zebra ventured down again to drink.

Once more Ngon and Ingala drove them towards the cubs, and the cubs came out from under the bushes. They managed better this time, and got near enough to the zebra to make funny little dashes at them. But the zebra kicked up their heels and galloped away. Again and again the same thing happened. The cubs couldn't bring off a hunt just yet. After all it was only their first lesson and the zebra knew all there was to know about hunting.

The cubs grew tired at last. Ngon and Ingala called to them and they all wandered off into the bush to rest in some nice shady place.

The zebra watched them go. Then, when everything seemed quite safe, they came down the sandy bank and stood in the pool, peacefully drinking.

At last the day came when Munya really *did* kill a buck. He had had a long, hard training before he was able to do so and had made the most dreadful mistakes. He had grown into a fine big cub with tremendously strong paws.

It was late afternoon; the lions were roaring terrifically: "Oo-oo-oo-ugh-ugh, rah-*oom*, rah-*oom*." There was no mistaking

those sounds, they were so fierce and wild. The lions were out to kill; they were hungry; they had not killed for three days.

Ngon and Imbube stood by the roadside. Farther along Ingala waited on the *veld* among thorn bushes, with the five cubs.

Thud-thud, thud-thud, and a herd of *impala,* chased by a lioness, came tearing along the road towards the lions. On seeing them the herd scattered, and one frantic *impala* bounded towards Ingala and the cubs among the thorn bushes. Munya dashed out, the *impala* dodged him and leaped over the bushes. But Ingala drove him back to Munya. She could easily have got the *impala* herself, but she wanted Munya, her cub, to have the chance—the glory of killing it.

Munya crouched and sprang to one side of the buck, then, running beside him a few paces, he leapt on to its back. The *impala* screamed. Munya struck its neck a tremendous blow with his paw, and the *impala* fell over at once and lay still, dead from a broken neck.

Lions kill like that, straight and clean. Munya rose from the *impala* and supper began at once. Snarling, spitting, growling, the lions and cubs threw themselves upon the dead body and pulled and tore at it.

Munya ran off with a delicious piece of flesh, and hidden under a bush, he devoured it. He was so afraid that one of the other lions might try and snatch it from him.

When he had finished he went back to the others, who snarled and growled at him. They wanted the rest of the *impala* for themselves. Munya managed to squeeze in amongst them, however, and grab a second helping.

Jackals stood round a little way from the kill, **barking**

Munya leapt on to the buck's back.

impatiently, waiting for the lions to finish, when they would get *their* share. Vultures with ugly skinny necks sat in the trees nearby ready to finish up anything that the jackals might leave. Odd-shaped grey figures, half laughing, half crying, hovered among the bushes farther away—hyenas, waiting until everyone else had finished when they would go and crack the bones and gnaw them.

It was dark by the time the lions had finished their supper and moved away from the kill.

Munya lay down by his mother, feeling very full and very comfortable. Ingala purred and gently washed him with her tongue; his face and paws were red with blood. She was proud of him. He had learnt the great lesson well, the way to kill, which to him meant his living.

IX.

Munya and Kulu go off on their own

At last the day came when Munya felt he must start off on his own. He was nearly four years old and wanted to see something of life for himself and have lots of fun and adventure. He had grown into a splendid young lion, a lovely fawn colour. His mane was black, someday to be as thick and long as his father's.

"Kulu!" he thundered, "Kulu!"

"Munya!" roared Kulu, coming across the *veld*, "Munya!"

Kulu had also grown into a fine young lion, but he had a brown mane. They had always been such friends; they *must* go off together. They were full of fun and mischief. They had nothing to do but enjoy themselves. They were like bachelor men, unmarried, with no one to worry about.

They went off roaring, roar upon roar, making as much noise as they could, just for fun.

All the other animals within hearing were frightened out of their wits, and tore away in every direction, which is exactly what the bachelor lions hoped they would do.

They then sharpened their claws, a thing that has to be attended to. A lion should keep his claws well sharpened when he goes off on his own, and has to hunt and kill for himself. They stood up on their hind-feet against the trunk of a tree, looking ridiculously tall. They drew their front claws down the trunk many

times. There was not much of the bark left when they had finished.

They strolled along happily across the *veld* and on to a road. Presently they came to the tennis court belonging to the ranger of that part of the Reserve. The bachelor lions gazed through the high wire netting which ran round it. They liked what they saw, particularly the tennis net itself, stretching across the centre of the court. It was something quite new to them. They must get in and play with it. They sniffed along the bottom of the wire netting until they came to a hole, just large enough for them to get through.

They stole across the court towards the net but on the way they found a small round thing lying on the ground, a tennis ball. Munya patted it with his paw. It rolled away towards Kulu, who patted it back. Munya picked it up in his jaws, dropped it and it bounced. The ball seemed like something alive to them, so they both ran after it and Kulu worried it and tore the outside covering off in strips. Munya bit the rubber part to pieces.

Having disposed of the ball they went up to the tennis net. Munya pulled at it, chewed it and settled down to make a really nice large hole in it. Kulu found a loose piece of rope to gnaw.

But they were not going to be allowed to have it *all* their own way. They saw some men animals watching them through the fence, but they did not look quite so harmless and gentle as they did when they were in the motor car things. They opened a gate and let a small white creature through. The creature came tearing towards them, barking and yapping, not in the least afraid of them.

The bachelor lions were so used to nearly every other animal being in a state of terror if they were anywhere near, that they were utterly taken aback at the fearlessness and daring of this alarming white creature. The men animals were coming towards them, too, one of them carrying a funny looking sort of stick.

Munya and Kulu lost their nerve and, not liking the look of things, they turned tail and hurried away. They found the hole at the bottom of the fence again, got through it and swung along the road at a good pace. The men animals and the white creature, a plucky little dog, walked back towards the gate.

Now Minung, the old baboon, was a little drunk that day. This sounds a shocking state for such a wise old baboon to be in. But it's true. He had slipped away from Baboonkop by himself, to a favourite marula tree, a tree that has yellow fruit rather like small plums. Some of it had fallen to the ground and Minung was sitting under the tree eating as much of it as he could, thoroughly enjoying himself. The fruit had been lying there in the heat for some time and was very much over-ripe. The juice had become as strong as wine, strong enough to make anyone drunk.

"Can't eat any more," hiccuped Minung at last, though he wished he could.

He stood up, swaying a little, and leant against the trunk of the tree for support. But it was too hot for him on the ground. He must get out of the sun. So he clambered up to a low-hanging branch, which was as high as he could manage. There he sat gently moving up and down, chuckling softly to himself, feeling very cheerful.

Just then a warthog came trotting towards the marula tree. His name was Gazan, and he was a fine stout fellow with beautifully curved tusks. He knew the tree well. Like Minung, he had slipped away by himself. When near the marula tree he slowed down and walked straight under it. He began eating the fruit, munching away. It was delicious.

Minung looked down at him and, feeling rather jolly, thought he'd have a bit of fun. He stretched out a long hairy arm, laid hold of Gazan's back and pinched it, a good hard pinch He hung on to it, too. Gazan, taken by surprise, shrieked and squealed with pain.

Munya and Kulu, not far away, heard the noise and wanted to know what it was all about. The bachelor lions, guided by Gazan's screams, pushed their way through thick bush and came out on to the grass. There they stood, watching, and a funny sight they saw: Minung, the old baboon, seated in the marula tree, bending down and pinching a warthog's back, the warthog struggling to get away.

Just then a large grey bird came and perched in a neighbouring tree, and cried with a harsh voice: "Go-way, go-way."

Minung saw the lions, barked, let go of Gazan and pulled himself higher up the marula tree.

"Go-way, go-way," screamed the bird again.

"I *will*," said Gazan to himself, also seeing the lions. He turned and tore off in the direction of his home, his tail, which had a funny little bunch of hair at the end of it, sticking straight up in the air.

The bachelor lions, having nothing else to do, couldn't

resist running after him. They had no thought of killing him, for they were not hungry. In any case it would hardly have been worth their while. A warthog is tough eating and his tusks are dangerous. They were only out for fun, to catch hold of his tail if they could, and play with it.

But Gazan knew all about bachelor lions. He knew how rough they were, and he never had been quite sure whether a lion would kill and eat a warthog, or not.

So he ran faster than he'd ever run before and kept a little way ahead of the lions. He knew that part of the *bushveld* better than they did. He dodged about and led them through tiresome prickly places. Their manes caught in thorn bushes and they were covered with prickles. At last, panting and breathless, he saw his wife and their little ones near a huge red antheap some yards farther on. The baby warthogs were playing round their mother, all their little tails, with tiny bunches of hair at the ends of them, sticking straight up.

Munya and Kulu were following closer now. Gazan could hear them crashing through the undergrowth behind him.

Mother Warthog must have seen them coming because suddenly, all in a moment, the baby warthogs disappeared through a hole into the antheap, she herself following. She must have gone in tail first, the way warthogs do, because Gazan could just see the tips of her tusks.

With a last tremendous effort he reached the antheap, but only just in time. The bachelor lions were at the point of snatching hold of his tail.

Mother Warthog backed farther down the hole to make room for Gazan, and he pushed his way in tail first, so that his

44

tusks faced the lions, ready to defend his family.

Munya and Kulu knew they were beaten. They were powerless against those fierce looking tusks, but they had had the fun of chasing and frightening the warthog. They strolled away from the big red antheap, leaving the warthog family safe inside. Tired after all their adventures, they threw themselves down to rest under a wild fig tree.

X.

Lizibulo

Lizibulo, a lovely young lioness, lay on a grassy mound under some trees one day. She had left the other lionesses with whom she had been going about; she was tired of them and preferred to be alone.

Along the road which ran past Lizibulo's mound, came Munya and Kulu. They were full-grown lions now. They had had all sorts of adventures and lots of fun. But they seemed to have sobered down a little as if they had more important things to do than just to amuse themselves.

It was spring time again and everything was fresh and green. Then Munya saw Lizibulo, and Lizibulo saw him. He was magnificent, every inch a king. By now he had a tremendous mane. It hung round his face and over his chest and shoulders.

The lions stopped and gazed at Lizibulo on her mound, graceful and dignified, like a queen on her throne. It was very hot, so they went and lay down under the trees near her.

All through the heat of the day they stayed there. When it was cooler Munya got up and began frisking about in front of Lizibulo, showing off a little perhaps. She came down from her throne and he patted her and played with her. She crossed the road on to the *veld* and sat there waiting for him.

Munya started towards her, Kulu with him. But Munya snarled and growled at him, and looked so fierce and angry that Kulu turned and walked away. Munya would have fought him if he had stayed. Lizibulo was Munya's chosen mate and wife; he would let no other lion come near her.

Kulu did not wish to fight his old pal, who was stronger and bigger than he was. Besides, he knew of several other young lionesses who would be only too pleased to see him.

Munya went up to Lizibulo and patted her again. She rubbed her head against his, and they moved away together, side by side, between the trees, into thick bush.

*   *   *

Three little lion cubs lay blinking at the sun one day with filmy blue eyes. Lizibulo, their mother, had brought them out of their lair on the ground floor of Baboonkop, for the first time. They stretched their little bodies and rolled over. They loved the warmth and sunshine. Lizibulo crooned to them and licked them.

"Miaow, miaow," mewed the cubs, "miaow, miaow, we like this; it's nicer than in the lair."

Munya came panting across the *veld* with a dead *wildebeeste*. He dropped it close to Lizibulo and the cubs. Lizibulo, who was ravenously hungry, began tearing at it at once; but Munya drove her off, growling. He dragged it away, set to and

made an enormous meal off it.   As father and master, it was his right to eat first.

When he had finished, Lizibulo went up to the *wildebeeste* and began her meal.   The cubs wobbled after her; their little legs were rather shaky.   They were too young to eat meat yet.

Munya, very red about the jaws and chest, lay cleaning himself. When she had finished devouring *wildebeeste,* Lizibulo took the cubs back to the lair and they cuddled up round her, purring little contented purrs.   It was time they went to bed.

Presently Munya got up and moved away. He stopped just below the Pulpit Rock.   Minung, the old baboon, looked down at him.   Perhaps he remembered the day he had first seen Munya, when as a little cub he had come walking across the *veld,* between his parents, to Baboonkop.   Now he saw Munya, fully grown, the finest black-maned lion in that part of the Reserve and—a father.

Munya gave out one long, deep roar, and strolled on. Minung clambered up the *kopje* to his cave.